MORNING WITH THE NEIGHBORS' BABY

Hastings, in his fuzzy pajamas, started to wail.

"As long as you're awake," said Mrs. Quayle, "would you mind watching Hastings while I get dressed and get breakfast started." She set him down solidly next to me.

Hastings howled and I felt like zipping him into the sleeping bag and sitting on him, but resisted the temptation. I reached out and put a firm hand on the seat of his fuzzy pajamas and held on.

Something was very, very wet. It was Hastings, and Hastings' pajamas. And now I suddenly realized: me, because I'd been holding on to him. A revolting situation, and one which would probably be repeated a thousand times more with our new baby. I didn't relish the prospect.

Time Flies!

Time Flies!

Florence Parry Heide

DRAWINGS BY MARYLIN HAFNER

A BANTAM SKYLARK BOOK®
TORONTO • NEW YORK • LONDON • SYDNEY • AUCKLAND

RL 5, 008–012

TIME FLIES!

A Bantam Book / published by arrangement with
Holiday House, Inc.

PRINTING HISTORY

Holiday House edition published October 1984
Bantam Skylark edition / October 1985

ISBN 0-553-15370-6

PRINTED IN THE UNITED STATES OF AMERICA
CW   0 9 8 7 6 5 4 3 2

With love to Chris—and to Jane!

Contents

Time Flies!

(1)

What Are These Elephants Doing in This Book?

I was just settling down in front of the world's biggest hot fudge sundae when I heard my mother saying no from a long way off. Or maybe it wasn't Mom after all, maybe it was the voice of my conscience because I'd been putting on so much weight that I couldn't button the shirts she'd bought me just last month for Christmas.

"Nooooo," echoed through the air, bounced off the walls of my room and into my head where it ricocheted around. That sundae was melting fast. I'd better finish it off while I could. Her voice was getting closer.

Just as I was reaching for a huge spoon, I heard *no* again, close and loud: *"Nooooo*-ah! Hurry up, you'll

3

be late for school." I opened my eyes. I was in bed. Another dream gone up in a puff of smoke. No hot fudge sundae was sitting in front of me after all, just another day of school.

It always takes me a long time to get awake in the morning, especially if I've been in the middle of a good dream. All I wanted to do was to put the pillow over my head, turn over, and get back to that hot fudge sundae. But it was too late.

"*Nooooo*-ah!"

"I'm up," I called back, but not loud enough and not fast enough. Mom was already opening the door. She'd probably have cardiac arrest when she saw the mess my room was in.

I reached under the pillow for my glasses and put them on. Without my glasses, Mom looked like a big blue balloon. With my glasses, she looked like a big blue balloon with fried hair on top. Usually she's pretty thin, but she was going to be having a baby next month.

"You slept through your alarm again," she said accusingly. "How can you keep doing that?"

"Practice," I told her, swinging my legs out of the bed and sitting up. As usual, I hit my head on the bunk bed above me. It's not that I need a bunk bed, there's only me. It's just that a built-in bunk bed was in my room when we'd moved in last year. I use the top part

for my clothes and everything else, including a lot of my drawings. I was practicing to be a comic-book artist. I'd also decided that I was going to write and illustrate joke books and riddle books. Right now I was working on a riddle book about elephants, *What Are These Elephants Doing in This Book?*

Maybe it would get to be a best-seller, and I'd get rich. Money was often on my mind because I'd figured out a long time ago that there must be easier ways of making money than doing a million jobs in and around the house for Dad.

This is the way I feel about money: it's only good if you can spend it for something you want to have or if it will get you out of something you don't want to do, like working.

This is the way Dad feels about money: it's only good if you can save it for some time in the future. *Save* it? For what? For when you're ninety-five and going on a hundred? Oh, wow.

I looked at the clock, blinked, and stood up. If I was late for school one more time I'd be called into the principal's office and maybe shot at sunrise. Sunset would be more convenient.

"Your room," said Mom despondently, looking around. "It looks like the ruins of an ancient, forgotten civilization."

"Comfy-looking place, isn't it?" I asked, fishing around on the top bunk for something to wear. Even by my own messy standards my room was messy.

"I've got a lot of homework to do," I explained. "And of course a lot of housework," I added cleverly. Both of those remarks were true.

The fact that my homework had mostly been to read comic books was beside the point.

As for housework: well, I spent a lot of time figuring out ways to get out of the jobs Dad lined up for me to do, and that was pretty time consuming.

Dad is an efficiency expert. That means he's pretty good at telling everyone else how to do things. That's his job at Weeble, Inc., which is a small company that makes mattresses. He's their time study expert. Who would want to spend his life figuring out faster ways to make mattresses? Dad.

"If you don't use time, time will use you." That's one of his favorite sayings. He has enough sayings to stretch around the world fifty-six times.

"I have to go to market this morning," said Mom sleepily. "We're out of everything. Anything special you'd like?"

"Food," I suggested. The last time she'd gone to market she came back with nothing but toothpaste and paper plates.

"Don't go back to bed," she warned.

"I hadn't thought of it, but it sounds like the best idea of the day," I said, yawning.

"It does, doesn't it?" asked Mom, brightening. She turned to go—back to bed, probably. "Hurry now, or you'll miss the bus again," she said over her shoulder.

I grabbed some pants and a shirt and headed for the bathroom. Since my room over the garage is separate from the rest of the house, it's sort of private. At least my parents don't come in very often, and that's lucky. This was the first time in ages that anyone but me had been in my room, anyone except Bib and Gabriel. They're our next-door neighbors. Bib's my age and she's a girl, although you wouldn't be able to tell it from the clothes she wears. Her real name is Roberta, but she doesn't look or act or sound or dress or seem like a Roberta.

Gabriel's her kid brother. There's a baby in the family, too, Hastings. So far, he wasn't old enough to get into my room. That would come, I predicted. And of course there would be Mom's new baby, too. I wouldn't have much privacy when he grew up. On the other hand, it would be someone else in the family to help with the chores.

But that was a long time off. I'd seen enough of Bib's baby brother, Hastings, to know that the crying, teething, drooling, dribbling, dripping, and diaper stage lasted a very long time, maybe forever. It would be a million years before Mom's baby would be old enough to help significantly around the house and yard.

I hadn't even finished brushing my teeth when I heard Bib pounding on the backdoor. *"Nooooo-*ah! Come on! Hurry up!"

Too much was happening for the first thing in the morning: people calling me, pushing me into the day before I was awake. Next it would be the bus, and after that school, and—

The bus. If I missed it, it would be another long, cold walk in the snow. I could hardly wait until the spring thaw when I could get back on my ten-speed bike.

I raced downstairs without bothering to comb my hair. Mom was nowhere in sight. There were a couple of apples on the kitchen counter. Apples it would be. I grabbed one, threw on my jacket, yelled to Mom that I was leaving, and dashed outside.

(2)

We Can't All Be Perfect

Bib was already running for the bus stop. With her long legs she looked sort of like a wishbone. I don't mind that she's so tall, it's just that I hate being shorter.

The bus stopped beside a huge snowbank. I slipped and slid and managed finally to climb on the bus right behind Bib. She was always ahead of me and I was always behind her. Sunrise, sunset.

"You made it," said Grace, the bus driver, in happy surprise.

"Sort of," said Bib, looking critically over her shoulder at me. I hadn't zipped up my jacket, and now I realized I had it on inside out. Maybe I'd start a new fad.

I followed Bib down the aisle while Grace put the bus in gear and eased out of the snowbank. I sat next to Bib, as usual, and as usual she kept talking.

"You forgot to comb your hair."

"I didn't forget," I said. "It was a conscious decision on my part. I weighed the options, examined the pros and cons, made a careful and considered judgment, and elected to leave it uncombed so it would look more natural. The natural look is in. But you can't be expected to know everything."

"Why don't you get up earlier?" she asked, as if it was her business.

"We can't all be perfect," I told her.

I started to eat my apple.

Bib nudged me. "Can't you read?" She pointed to the front of the bus. A hand-lettered sign read, "No food, except for thought." Grace was always putting up signs.

I leaned my head back and closed my eyes, chewing my apple and contemplating life.

Bib nudged me again. "Have your parents decided on a name for the baby yet?"

I thought for a minute. "You've seen those restaurants and boats and taverns that are combination names?" I asked. "You know, if the owner is named Ronald and his wife is named Louise, they call it Ron-

Lou? Well, that's a strong possibility. My father's name is Walter and Mom's name is Mary. They may call the baby Wal-Mar."

"Or Mar-Wal," said Bib quickly. "There's no reason the father's name has to be first in a situation like that. In fact, since most families have such antiquated ideas that they give the baby the father's last name instead of the mother's, it's only right that—"

I knew just where this conversation was heading. Actually, I didn't know what they had decided to call the baby. I'd read somewhere that some tribes of Indians used to name a baby for the first thing a mother saw when he was born, names like Crooked Tree or Half Moon. I wondered if Mom had read that, too, and maybe name the baby Dr. Fessner, or maybe Ceiling or Door.

Bib nudged me again. At this rate I'd be black and blue by the end of the day.

"Don't go back to sleep. If you do, you'll be crabby all day. Besides, I want to talk. It's too jouncy to read on the bus. Did you finish the report for Mr. Dooster?"

"The report." I groaned.

"Stop snoring," said Bib. "Did you do the report or not?"

"Of course, Mother," I lied.

"It's due today, you know."

"I know." Well, I knew it now. I'd forgotten all about it. In Bruce Dooster's class in American Literature we'd been studying comic books. Our report on the course ("Comic Books: Their Role in American Literature") was due today. A lot of our grade would depend on it, so I'd have to write it this morning.

Not that I usually worry too much about homework or about grades, but I really needed an *A* in American Literature because my other grades weren't very exciting and Dad really likes exciting grades. He likes them so much that if I didn't get at least a *B* average, I couldn't ride my bike this spring, and a bike that can't be ridden is worse than no bike at all.

Well, I'd have to write the report on comic books in math class, which meant that I'd get that much farther behind in math, which meant that I'd be so far behind I could never catch up.

I wished for the hundredth time that I could be home in bed. I think better in a horizontal position. Maybe there was something to be said for Weeble mattresses after all.

Bib and I were the last ones off the bus because Bib created a scene about my dropping the apple core on the floor of the bus. Just to keep the noise level down, I put it in my pocket, and since my jacket was inside out the pocket was hard to get to.

The day was starting off in a pretty dumb way, which is the way most of my days start. "I wish it could be tomorrow," I muttered as I stepped off the bus into more snow.

"We can't have tomorrow without today," said Grace.

This was going to be a long day. I could tell.

(3)

All You Need Is a Little Confidence

In math class, first hour, Mr. Dobbs put a whole lot of problems on the board and told us to work them out. Then he sat down and picked up a book. I decided it might be fun to be a teacher, getting kids to do all the work while you lounged around reading.

I started to write my report on comic books for Bruce Dooster. Every once in a while, Mr. Dobbs would look up from his book and glance around the room and each time he looked, he saw me scribbling busily away, so when class was over and I handed in a blank sheet of paper, he looked sort of surprised. At least I'd finished the report, and I walked into American Literature class with a light heart and with Bib right ahead of me, whistling.

Bruce Dooster was wearing a bright red shirt with a black bow tie and black suspenders, and with his droopy mustache he looked sort of like an old-fashioned fireman.

Bib sat a couple of rows behind me, a built-in spy. Pacing up and down, snapping his suspenders, Bruce Dooster started to talk. "Our unit on comic books is done, fini, over, complete, kaput," he announced, "except for your grades, which will be forthcoming as soon as I have examined your papers, which I will proceed to do promptly. Be sure to pick up your own comic books on your way out of class."

Everyone had brought his own supply of comic books for Bruce Dooster to look at and discuss in class. My own collection was in a big blue canvas bag, and I could see it beside his desk.

I glanced over the paper I'd written in math class. There wasn't much of it, and what there was consisted mostly of quotes from Bruce Dooster. That's the best way to get a good grade: quote the teacher. They love to see their remarks in print.

"And now, if you will pass your reports to the front of the room, I will collect them."

Everybody passed their reports to the guy in front

of them and then he passed them ahead to the next guy. That's how I got to see Bib's report, which was about as thick as the New York telephone directory.

I looked behind me. She was looking smug. It was demoralizing to be in the same class with a workaholic. No matter what I would ever do, she would do it better and faster.

"So," Bruce Dooster said, "so much for comic books and their place in American Literature."

He snapped his suspenders.

"You have probably discovered in this class that the ability to read, while commendable and convenient, is not really essential if we confine ourselves to comic books. We can tell what the story is about just by looking at the pictures. Easy! No complicated reading skills are required. That simplifies life, to be sure, and that is the American way."

He walked up and down, snapping his suspenders.

"Now there is another form of modern American literature which also entertains. It also demands no skills on our part. I refer to television, and television is what we will study next.

"Anyone born today," he said, and I thought of the baby, "will not be thrust into the old world of Walt Whitman and Nathaniel Hawthorne, once our most revered writers. No, his world will be—"

Comic Books and American Literature

He paused, pained, and his eyes focused behind me. I knew without turning around that it was Bib. I turned around, anyway. It was.

Her hand waved madly. "Yes?" asked Bruce Dooster. He'd told us at the beginning of the year that he was always open to questions, and Bib always had one.

She spoke in a loud, clear voice. "When you say 'his world will be,' Mr. Dooster, you mean to say 'his or her world,' don't you?"

"Let me phrase it this way," he said. "Babies born today will find the written word largely supplanted by the spoken, televised word."

People like Bib and people like teachers would rather talk than listen.

Actually, I already knew a lot about television, although I hadn't had a chance to watch much lately because the set is in the living room and that's where Dad usually is, at least after he gets home from work. And Dad thinks that television is a waste of time.

Anyway, something was wrong with the set and the repairman couldn't come for a few days.

Bruce Dooster kept walking up and down and talking. "Time marches on. We must keep adjusting to change. Here in this class we are preparing for the future. If you want to dig up the past, sign up for Mrs. Smeed's class in archaeology or Miss Ribble's class in classics."

Bib again. Bruce Dooster took a deep breath before saying, "Yes?"

"*Miss* is out-dated," said Bib primly. "*Ms.* is the acceptable term."

He smiled. "*Ms.* Ribble," he corrected himself. He made it sound like *Miserable,* but I guess Bib was satisfied because that was her last interruption.

At the end of the period, Bruce Dooster handed out mimeographed sheets. "These are the terms with which I want you to become familiar in our study of television," he announced. "Naturally, the best way to learn anything is by first-hand experience. When you watch any of these categories, put a check next to the type of program you have seen. You must watch at least one of everything on the list. Of course, if you watch more, you will get extra credit, just as you would get extra credit for reading additional books in another class."

I glanced at the paper. It was a chart with terms like COMMERCIAL, TALK SHOW, STATION BREAK, SOAP OPERA, CRIME DRAMA, SIT-COM, DOCU-DRAMA, and so on, and spaces to check next to them.

On the way out of class, I picked up my big bag of comic books and put it in my locker. I had the best comic book collection in the class, maybe in the world.

Certainly it was the *heaviest*.

The day yawned ahead, and I do mean yawned. And lunch in the cafeteria was something spooky inside of stale buns and something that looked like little jellyfish, so I'd be happy to get through the day and home to our refrigerator. Mom would have been to market and back by now. That apple seemed about ten years ago. Even the core, mellowing in my jacket pocket in my locker, was beginning to look good to me.

On the bus on the way home, Grace sang loudly:

"Straight ahead, head, head, on the road,
        road, road,
Straight ahead and you'll never go wrong."

"It might be fun for you to be a bus driver when you grow up," I said to Bib, who was sitting next to me as usual. "I mean driveress," I added.

Bib sighed loudly. "I am grown-up. And my birthday's in a couple of weeks. I'll be another year older and I haven't accomplished anything. I'm *stag*nating."

"You won't be another year older, just another day," I said reassuringly. "Besides, think of all the presents you'll get."

"I am thinking of them. Socks which will be the wrong size, shape, color, and consistency. A handmade sweater in some obscure, obscene color, with my initials on it, which won't fit me and wouldn't fit anyone. Handkerchiefs with my name embroidered on them. Handkerchiefs," she repeated scornfully. "And personalized stationery with cute designs."

She sighed despondently. "Things with names or initials on them can't be given to someone else, you know."

I guessed what she had in mind: giving *me* the presents she hadn't wanted for *my* birthday. I was glad everything she was going to get would be personalized.

"All I really want is a skateboard," she confided morosely. "But I'll never get it."

"A skateboard," I echoed, impressed. "That would be pretty tricky up on that hill we call home."

I was afraid to *try* a skateboard. Or anything else. "I'm just not the athletic type," I told her.

"Nonsense. All you need is a little confidence. And a little practice. And you can do anything."

"I'm not going to try a skateboard until I've learned how," I said.

Bib sighed again. "I might as well stop thinking about it," she said. "I'll just make myself miserable, especially when I open that box of cutesy stationery."

I hadn't thought about Bib's birthday and about how I'd probably have to give her a present, especially if I wanted her to give *me* a present when *my* birthday rolled around, which it would be doing soon.

As a matter of fact, if I'd thought about her birthday at all, which I hadn't, I'd probably have given her cute personalized stationery. Now I'd have to think of something else.

She'd mentioned handkerchiefs. Maybe I could get her a nice box of Kleenex.

(4)

Talk About
Over-Achievers!

Gabriel, Bib's kid brother, had been watching for the bus, as usual. When Bib and I got off, he picked his way over the snow towards me.

"It's code," he said.

Gabriel has trouble with his L's and R's, so he can't even pronounce his own name.

"You think this is cold," I told him. "Last year it was so cold that I couldn't blow out the candles on my birthday cake. The flames were frozen. I had to break them off, one at a time."

He looked at me with his round eyes that always got rounder when he was thinking. He doesn't say very much. Still waters wun deep.

"Golly gee whillikers," said Bib sarcastically.

"Gowwy gee whiwwikehs," echoed Gabriel. He picks up new expressions pretty fast.

"Come on, Gabriel," said Bib, starting over towards their house which was a carbon copy of our house. "We'll be late for class."

More classes! As if she hadn't had enough for one day. Her family is so scheduled that if they don't carry programs around with them they don't know what they're doing. Talk about over-achievers! Bib often took classes after school and sometimes on Saturdays. And even though Gabriel was still too young to go to regular school, they had enrolled him in all sorts of classes. Name it, they took it. Maybe ball-bouncing or quilting or fingernail improvement, who knows. Who *cares*, I told myself, but what all this meant to me was that there was no one to talk to after school.

Bib had already walked ahead of Gabriel and me towards their house. I set my bag of comics down, made a snowball, threw it after her and missed. She turned around, made a face and a snowball, threw the snowball, and got me right in the head. If you want to get an inferiority complex in a hurry, spend some time with Bib.

"Speaking of birthday cakes," I said to Gabriel, "I hear that Bib's going to be having a birthday. Your mom will probably make her a personalized birthday cake."

Gabriel nodded. "I have to buy a pwesent," he said glumly.

"And you can't think of anything, right?" I said. "How about some cute personalized stationery? Or if you think that's too mundane, how about a mink coat with her initials?"

"I don't have any money," said Gabriel very distinctly. It's only the *L*'s and *R*'s that give him trouble.

"Then you'll have to think of a way to make money," I told him. "You could take care of that baby brother, for instance. And we're going to be having a baby in our family, too, pretty soon. You could have a baby-sitting *service*."

Gabriel shook his head. "Mom says I'm too wittle."

"Oh. Well, there are lots of other ways to make money. Snowballs, for instance," I said, making one.

He looked at me seriously.

"Snowballs could mean big business. You could make hundreds and hundreds of dollars. You could be financially independent. You could buy *two* presents for Bib."

I threw my snowball in the direction of Quayles' house, and hit it. All I really need is a big stationary target.

"You've heard of lemonade stands, perhaps," I went on. "In the summer, kids all over America make a bundle of money. But what happens when winter comes? They give up. It never seems to occur to them that they could prosper in the cold months with a different product."

His big round eyes got bigger and rounder.

"Ever think of selling ready-made snowballs?" I asked. "Small, medium, large, and of course economy size. People wouldn't have to make their own snowballs, they could come to your stand and buy yours. You'd be swamped with customers. You'd make a fortune."

He stood watching me while I made another snowball.

"I know what you're going to say," I went on. "You're going to say that if it's such a great idea, how come there aren't snowball stands all over the place, just the way there are lemonade stands and Kool-Aid stands in the summer. Well, the reason you don't see any snowball stands is that no one has thought of it before. Not until today." I held up my hand. "Don't thank me. My reward is in knowing that I have started

GABRIELS SNOWBALL
EMPORIUM

SM MED LG

you on a lifetime career. The strength of this idea lies
in the fact that it needs no capital investment. You can
start any time. You can start," I said earnestly, "today.
This very afternoon."

"Gabriel! Come on!" Bib had opened their backdoor
and was standing there. It was just luck that I happened
to have a snowball in my hand. This time I didn't miss.
She slammed the door.

Glowing with satisfaction, I turned back to Gabriel.
"You could be a real businessman," I told him, "A real
entrepreneur."

He kept looking at me.

"An entrepreneur, as of course you know," I went
on, "is a person who organizes, operates, and assumes
the risk for business ventures." I'd memorized the def-
inition last month. I hurried on. "What risk, you ask,
with a business venture like this, a snowball stand?
Well, the obvious risk of an unexpected thaw. However, this risk can be minimized by being prepared to
transfer your snowballs at a moment's notice to the
freezer. Naturally, you will then have a head start on
any competitors. You'll have snowballs long after theirs
have melted. You'll make so much money you can
buy everyone in your *family* a present. Everyone in the
world."

I picked up my bag of comics. "You listen to my

advice and you'll be able to retire when you're ten years old," I said. "You'll never have to work again."

Gabriel looked at me for a minute. Then he reached down to make a snowball. I started to walk over to our house.

(5)

Oh, Let's Not Be Hasty

I walked in the backdoor, calling, "I'm home, Mom."
No answer. I hung up my inside-out jacket and headed
for the refrigerator.

I could see at a glance that Mom had forgotten to
go to market. No sign of her: she was probably taking
a nap—after all, she was sleeping for two.

I'd have a couple of hours before Dad got home
from work. I was a free bird, but there was nothing I
really wanted to do. It was too bad the television set
wouldn't be fixed until next week: I could have been
working on homework for Bruce Dooster.

I knew Dad's list of chores for me to do would be

on a pad on the kitchen counter. I'd have to think up an excuse to have missed seeing it. There were lots of possibilities, especially in a kitchen as haphazard as ours. Dad would run out of jobs before I ran out of excuses.

I sat down at the counter and tried to draw my latest elephant riddle:

> What did the elephant say when he saw a
> hippopotamus in his bathtub?

> *You look silly in that bathing suit.*

I was getting pretty good at elephants, but I hadn't tried a hippopotamus before.

I tried to draw a hippo in a tub, but so far it looked sort of like a hot dog in a bun. That made me hungrier than ever. Maybe I'd have to settle for a big bowl of catsup.

I was opening and closing the cupboard doors, looking for possibilities, when Mom came wandering into the kitchen, looking the way she usually did the first thing in the morning except that this was the last thing in the afternoon.

"Hi, Mom," I said cheerfully, "want something to eat? There's a bag of flour here that we could probably whip into something tasty."

She smiled and sat down on one of the kitchen stools.

If she got any bigger and heavier, we'd have to get some stronger furniture. The stool wobbled danger-ously.

The pad with Dad's instructions for me was in plain sight, so I spoke quickly. "Dad's left a list of chores here for me but I can't read his writing. Too bad."

"Better call him at the office," said Mom.

Call him at the office! Asking Dad what he wanted me to do would be just like asking the dentist to do a little extra drilling.

"Oh, let's not be hasty," I said, stalling for time.

"I think I'm going to be having a baby," Mom said conversationally.

"Yes, so I've heard," I said. "And it's going to be great having another kid around here to share the work load." I talked fast so she'd forget about my calling Dad. "Although, actually, I've figured it out, and he won't be old enough to help significantly with mowing the grass or shoveling the snow for 4,176 days. I've broken that down into hours and weeks and years, too, and it all adds up to a long time."

"I'm sure he can hardly wait to get started," said Mom. "In fact, he's decided to come now instead of later. At least my labor pains have started, and that's usually a sign of something going on."

I stared. The baby, now?

It was the first time I could remember that I was anxious to get in touch with Dad. I didn't want Mom to have the baby right here right now, with just me around to deliver it. And I couldn't drive her to the hospital. I was at that awkward age, too old to take a nap, too young to drive.

I reached for the telephone.

"What's the number?" I asked, trying to stay calm.

"Look it up," she said. "I can't remember anything at the moment, including your name or mine."

I grabbed the telephone book and flipped through the pages. *W, W, W,* for Weeble, Inc.

I dialed and after a couple of rings someone answered and said *WeBlink,* because that's what Weeble, Inc., sounds like.

I asked for Dad and waited.

"Mr. Langren's office."

That made Dad sound pretty important. This must be his secretary.

"Could I please speak to Mr. Langren?" I asked.

"May I ask who's calling?" asked the voice.

"Yes, his son," I told her.

"I'm sorry, Miss Yessison, but he's stepped out of the office for a moment. Would you like to hold?"

I could see I'd have to try to sound more like an adult.

I nodded, realized she couldn't see me unless she had X-ray eyes, and finally mumbled yes in a somewhat deeper voice.

"They put me on hold," I whispered to Mom.

"I wish they could do the same for me," said Mom.

I swallowed. Maybe the baby would just pop out, here and now.

I cleared my throat nervously.

"Don't worry," said Mom. "It takes a while to get the baby from where it is to here."

"We can only hope that the baby's read the same books you have," I told her. "If he's anything like Dad, he'll figure out some way to save time."

Mom stood up. "I'll get my suitcase. Dad packed it three months ago. It's got everything in it but the kitchen sink, and we probably won't need that."

While Mom was getting her suitcase and while I was on hold, I practiced saying hello in a deep voice. I was so absorbed in my progress that when Dad answered, I jumped.

"Yes, Miss Yessison," he said.

I was tempted to tell him that the preferred salutation was Ms., but held my tongue.

"It's Noah," I said.

"Noah? What about him, Miss Yessison?" he asked. "Is anything wrong? Are you calling from school?"

I sighed. "Dad, it's me, Noah."

"Noah, I was on the line with another party, a Miss Yessison from school, and I'll have to put you on hold."

Being put on hold was getting to be pretty popular. While I waited, I stretched the phone as far as it would go and opened another of the kitchen cupboards. Zilch.

Finally Dad came back on the line. "I was just talking to someone from your school, Noah, and we must have been cut off. Are you in some kind of trouble over there? Who is this Miss Yessison? Is she a counselor?"

Talking to Dad was like going the wrong way on a one-way street.

"I'll have to get to the bottom of it when I get home," said Dad.

"Actually," I said, "the reason I'm calling is about the baby."

"What baby? Don't try to divert me, Noah."

Mom came back into the kitchen, setting her suitcase down with a thud. "Good heavens, are you still talking to Dad?" she asked.

I shrugged helplessly, and she reached for the phone. "Walter, it's me. No, I'm not at the school. I'm here, at home, and I want you to drive me over to the hospital."

A pause, during which Mom sighed. "Yes, Walter,

now. I've already called Dr. Fessner." Mom sighed
again. It was impossible not to when you were engaged
in a conversation with Dad.

"Yes, I know it's ahead of schedule, and I've tried
to explain that to the baby, but apparently the right
timing is the farthest thing from his or her mind. Just
come home now." Another pause, another sigh. "Fifteen minutes. My contractions are fifteen minutes
apart." She glanced up at the clock. "Make that twelve."

I knew it would take Dad exactly twenty-eight and
a half minutes to get home from the office and exactly
fourteen and three-quarter minutes to get from home
to the hospital. He'd been practicing by making a lot
of dry runs and timing them all. He always does things
that way. The fastest way to the office, the market,
the gas station, the bathroom.

I wished he'd get here pretty soon. I don't usually
wish for Dad's arrival. This was the exception that
proved the rule. Mom and I sat staring at the clock,
something Dad would consider a waste of time. But
what else was there to do? Neither of us could get our
minds on anything but the impending appearance of
the baby.

"How do you feel?" I asked, just to keep the conversation going.

"Just the way I felt when you started coming," she

said. "It's sort of hard to describe. You'll never know because you'll never have a chance to have a baby. So much for equal opportunity."

She stood up and shuffled around the kitchen. "I feel as if I've been pregnant for a hundred years," she said. "There ought to be an easier way."

"Instant babies," I agreed. "They'll come in a powdered form. Just add hot water and stir."

"We'd better call Quayles', tell them you'll be coming sooner than we'd expected."

We'd planned a long time ago that I'd stay over there when the baby came, and I'd been looking forward ever since to the prospect of three terrific meals a day. Mrs. Quayle is a great cook, whereas Mom never seems to get the connection between food and stoves.

"Noah," she said, "do you think I've been a good mother? Because here I am, doing it again."

"Of course you're a good mother," I told her. "Otherwise how would I have turned out to be such a great guy?"

"I hope I get another one like you," she said.

I looked up at the clock. Six and a half minutes before Dad would arrive. I called Quayles' and Bib answered.

"Congratulations," I said. "You have won our mystery guest, and he will be on your doorstep within the hour. He needs no special care, just lots to eat. Please inform the management."

"What's happening?" asked Bib.

"The baby," I said. "He's decided that the moment has arrived."

"Oh, wow. I'll tell Mom." She hung up.

A screeching of brakes, a honking of horn. Dad.

"Twenty-five and a half minutes," he announced as he swept through the door. "I cut three minutes off the time. All set to go? Feeling all right? I have everything under control, there's nothing to worry about, don't panic."

"Who's panicking?" asked Mom, getting her coat.

"Have you been filling in the chart?" asked Dad.

"The chart," echoed Mom. "No, as a matter of fact, I forgot all about it."

"But we have to have it! It's essential!" said Dad. He sprinted off to their bedroom.

Dad can't even brush his teeth without a chart.

"Which chart?" I asked.

"He made a chart and I was supposed to start filling it in when I started labor. Onset of pains, duration of pains, strength of same, interval between same, additional signs and symptoms. He doesn't think I can have the baby unless we fill in the spaces."

"A baby without a chart?" I asked, throwing up my hands in a horrified way. "Surely you jest."

She looked at the clock again. "Who was the nut who said 'time flies'?" In a louder voice, she said, "Walter, forget about the chart. Let's go."

He raced in from the bedroom. "I remember now. I had packed it in your suitcase. A place for everything, and everything in its place. It's as simple as that."

"Good. Then we're all set. You bring the suitcase, I'll bring the baby." She hugged me good-bye. "We'll call you at Quayles'," she said.

"About your problem with the school, Noah," said Dad. "I'll want to hear about it when all this excitement is over. First, identify the problem. Then, figure out the solution. Problems don't solve themselves, you know."

"I know." I waved them off. When they came back, there would be three of them. It was a mind-boggling thought.

It wasn't until they'd gone that I realized they'd taken my canvas bag of comics instead of Mom's suitcase. Well, they'd have something to read while they were waiting for the baby, anyway.

(6)

Babies Are Pretty Boring

I rolled my pajamas, a change of clothes, and some supplies into my sleeping bag and put Bruce Dooster's television-watching chart in my pocket. I could get in some pretty good television time at Quayles'. Then I locked up the house and started through the snow over to Bib's house.

"Oh, isn't it exciting about the baby?" asked Mrs. Quayle when I arrived at their backdoor. She was trying to feed her own baby and dabs of disgusting-looking vegetables were all over him, the high chair, the floor, and Mrs. Quayle. And whatever she had just succeeded in getting into his mouth was already dribbling repulsively down his receding chin.

Not a very attractive sight. And it would be months before our new baby would be even this far along. Babies are pretty boring, and they can't do anything for themselves. I just hoped no one expected me to feed ours or change it or pay much attention to it.

"Mr. Quayle's off on a business trip," said Mrs. Quayle. "And Bib and Gabriel are in the living room, I believe. Just go right in. Dinner won't be ready for an hour or so."

My heart sank. So did my stomach. "But there are potato chips and dip and pretzels in there to tide you over."

Maybe I could board here for a couple of years. I glanced around the kitchen. Something was bubbling on the stove, something was baking in the oven, a pie was on the counter, and I knew from experience that the refrigerator was stuffed with food.

I walked into the living room with my sleeping bag. I'd be sleeping in here. I could watch television all night if I wanted to.

Gabriel was lying on the floor looking at a program and trying to shake some money out of a piggy bank. Bib was nowhere in sight. Another plus: more food, fewer lectures for me. I helped myself to a handful of pretzels.

"Hi, Gabriel," I said. "What are you watching?"

"A pwogwam," he said.

I looked at it for a minute, munching pretzels.

Sometimes any program is better than no program at all, but this wasn't one of those times. It was a roundtable medical discussion about fallen arches.

"You know why they're called panel discussions?" I asked. "Because sometimes the participants are made of wood. Wooden panels carved to look like real people."

He kept shaking his piggy bank, trying to shake out some coins.

"Instead of working so hard at trying to get pennies out of a piggy bank, you could be working on your business ventures. You'll have your snowball stand, of course, but you'll still have time for more money-making enterprises. I have other ideas I will be happy to share at no cost to you."

He turned around to look at me.

"You could raise canaries, for instance," I told him. "Just buy a package of birdseed and plant it. There's a lot of money in selling canaries, you know."

"They'd fwy away," he said.

"Not if you planted the seeds in cages."

He regarded me thoughtfully and then he turned back to the television set. So much for my Neilsen rating.

Bib came down the stairs, wearing a towel wrapped around her head, a big ugly old bathrobe which had probably been her father's, and huge fuzzy slippers.

"A really tasteful costume," I told her. "Clothes make the person, an expression I have coined only tonight. In fact, I may copyright it, get royalties. Shakespeare isn't the only pebble on the beach, you know. I, too, can make up sayings that will echo through the ages."

Bib unwound the towel that was wrapped around her head and her long wet hair fell limply over her shoulders.

"Haven't you anything better to do than to watch this dumb program?" she asked.

"I happen to be getting credit for it," I told her. "I'll probably be the only one in class who's watched a panel discussion about a distressful situation, i.e., fallen arches."

"Huh," she said, but I noticed that she started to watch it, too. Well, this was one class I could get a better mark in than Bib. I could outwatch her any time. She had other hobbies. I didn't, except for my drawing, and I could do that while I watched. That's more than you can say for piano playing, for instance.

The program finally droned to a close and the commercial came on. I got out my chart and checked it.

PANEL DISCUSSION, check. COMMERCIAL, check.

That was the end of any concentrated viewing because Mrs. Quayle brought Hastings in for us to admire and watch. He couldn't walk yet, but he could get around and pull himself up on things that fell down and put things in his mouth that should come out, and it took all of us to keep an eye on him. It was like a preview of coming attractions. I wasn't looking forward to this particular stage of our baby, or in fact any stage that I could think of. A good invention would be to have babies get born when they're five or six or something.

Finally dinner was ready.

"The way to a man's heart is through his stomach," I whispered to Bib as we sat down at the table. "Or, to put it more succinctly, the way to a person's heart is through his or her stomach."

We had roast beef with potatoes and other things that went with roast beef and potatoes, a far cry from the bowl of catsup I had visualized just a few hours earlier. For dessert (dessert!) we had apple pie and ice cream. I wondered if they could start a carryout service.

After dinner there was all the excitement about getting the baby, Hastings, settled for the night and getting the dishes settled in the dishwasher, then there was all the excitement about a phone call from the hospital

from Dad. Dad calling me—that was a first. He said that everything was proceeding according to schedule, whatever that meant, and that Mom was doing fine, whatever *that* meant.

After the telephone call, we tried to watch television, but since Hastings had decided against bed and in favor of the living room, it meant that although we were *watching* television, the sound track was mostly Hastings. Maybe I could get credit for one situation comedy, anyway.

The peace and quiet of our own house was starting to seem very attractive, but at the moment that I had *that* thought I had another: our house would be neither peaceful nor quiet nor attractive again for many years. Well, this was probably good practice for what lay ahead.

Finally everyone went to bed, leaving me with the sleeping bag, a cold salami sandwich, and a warm television set. I sighed happily and settled down to watch a crime drama. I'd be getting extra credit for the show and for all the commercials and station breaks. I got out Bruce Dooster's chart and started to fill it in.

I Knew My Moments
Were Numbered

It was the middle of the night. I'd fallen asleep with the television set on and the screen was lighted but blank. I was just reaching up to turn it off when a large furry animal landed on my stomach.

Oh, wow. I tried to push it aside so I could escape from my sleeping bag, but the creature floundered around on top of me. It was either a small vicious wild animal that had found its way into the house, or else it was an attack dog looking for the jugular. I knew my moments were numbered.

My heart was in my mouth, my glasses were nowhere to be found—they'd probably fallen off in my sleep. Well, I'd never need them again unless they decided to bury me with them on.

The lights blazed on. Maybe it was a burglar and he'd brought along a bloodhound to sniff out the jewels, the silver, and the money. He could have all I owned, as far as I was concerned. What's thirty-five cents, really, when it's a matter of life and death?

I rubbed my eyes. The furry creature was staring at me greedily. I felt around cautiously for my glasses and put them on.

"Don't mind us, dear," said Mrs. Quayle. "Hastings loves to get up early in the morning, don't you, sweetums?"

Hastings, in his fuzzy pajamas, started to wail.

"Now, now, it's only Noah," said Mrs. Quayle, picking him up. "He didn't recognize you, Noah, without your glasses."

"I didn't recognize him, either, without them," I told her. Now I was wide awake, with enough adrenalin coursing through my system to last the rest of the week.

I looked at my watch. Six o'clock. I'd been right. It *was* the middle of the night.

"We're sorry if we got you awake, aren't we, sweetums?" cooed Mrs. Quayle. If sweetums was sorry, he didn't look it. He looked smug.

"Oh, that's all right," I lied politely. "I'm an early riser myself."

"That's nice," said Mrs. Quayle, hanging onto Hastings, who was squirming madly. "As long as you're awake anyway, would you mind watching Hastings while I get dressed and get breakfast started, there's a dear." She set him down solidly next to me and Hastings started to scream.

"He usually cries for a while in the morning, it's nothing to be alarmed about," she said as she left me. "He'll be all right once he's had something to eat."

And I'd be all right once I got back to sleep. Hastings howled and I felt like zipping him into the sleeping bag and sitting on him, but resisted the temptation. I reached out and put a firm hand on the seat of his fuzzy pajamas and held on, then I leaned back and closed my eyes. What this family needed was a playpen or a zookeeper.

I was sure I had never gone through this particular phase as a baby, getting awake at the crack of dawn, ready to roll. He kept screaming. Maybe I'd feel better if I screamed for a while, too.

Something was very, very wet. It was Hastings, and Hastings' pajamas. And now I suddenly realized: me, because I'd been holding onto him. A revolting situation, and one which would probably be repeated a thousand times more with our new baby. I didn't relish the prospect.

By the time we were sitting down at breakfast, I was

somewhat mollified. Pancakes and sausages. So I was awake a little earlier than usual, so what.

I was just having my last bite when the telephone rang. Mrs. Quayle went into the living room to answer it. "Noah," she said, smiling, when she came back to the kitchen, "it's for you, and it's good news."

At home, I never got phone calls. Here, I was Mr. Popular.

It was Mom. She'd had the baby in the middle of the night.

"It's a girl," she said.

"Oh, well, I guess it had to be one or the other." And it was certainly better than one of each.

"Leslie Laura," she told me. "Isn't it a beautiful name? Leslie Laura Langren."

I tried to imagine Gabriel trying to say *that* one. Weswee Wauwa Wangwen.

"What does she look like?" I asked to be polite. Babies all look alike, but you can't tell their mothers that, especially if it's *your* mother.

"Just the way you looked when you were born. Sort of prunish. Makes a lot of noise, too, just the way you did. You can come over to the hospital tonight, look at her through a glass window, since you have a cold."

A cold? That was *last* month. Having a baby hadn't improved Mom's memory.

"Mrs. Quayle invited Dad over there for dinner,"

added Mom. "Isn't that nice? So after dinner he can bring you over to see the baby. And me. Then he'll take you back to Quayles' for the night, all right?"

"Great," I said. Naturally I'd rather stay at Quayles' than in our house with Dad who would probably dream up chores for me to do.

"Well, Dad's gone home for some sleep, which he didn't get any of last night, you can be sure. Then he's going to the office. He's going to pass out cigars. Isn't that something?"

We talked for another minute or so, and I said congratulations a couple of times. I'm not very conversational on a telephone.

When I told everyone at the breakfast table about the baby, Bib said, "I'm glad it's a girl. One more woman in the world to help fight for our rights."

Well, I'd be around to see that *Bib* wasn't around to brainwash my sister.

Mrs. Quayle was spooning something ugly into Hastings' mouth. "A new little girl, think of that. What's her name?"

"Leslie Laura Langren."

"Leslie," said Bib. "Good. She could be a girl or boy, a man or woman, with a name like that. No one will be deciding anything about her in advance because of her name."

The broken record.

I took one last bite of sausage and went into the living room to roll up my sleeping bag. It was time to make the run for the bus.

"I see it's starting to snow," I said to Gabriel, pointing out of the window. "Lucky you, getting to stay home. You're one of the few people in this country who is in a position to make a startling scientific discovery. Everyone else is either in school or working or watching television or doing housework. You and you alone have the opportunity to observe and record something that has never been observed or recorded before."

I rolled up the sleeping bag and stuck it behind a big chair in the corner.

"Of course there's not much money in science, but there's a lot of recognition. You'd be in all the books."

I started putting on my jacket, right side out this time.

"You know what scientists say about snowflakes. No two alike. But how do they really know for sure? Is anyone out examining each and every snowflake, putting the theory to the acid test? No. You could be famous. Your birthday could be a national holiday. And all you need to do is to find two snowflakes that are identical."

He glanced at the television set and back at me. I

knew he was torn between turning it on and finding twin snowflakes.

"Ridiculous as it seems, no one is now embarked on that journey of proof. No one but you, if you are willing to undertake this assignment." I clapped him on the shoulder. "You'd be a child prodigy, and you know what that means."

"Come on," called Bib, "it's time for the bus."

She was ahead of me, as usual, and I hurried to catch up.

(8)

Win Some, Lose Some

Win some, lose some: I got an *F* on the math quiz Mr. Dobbs had given us yesterday and I got an *A* on my comic book report for Bruce Dooster. The good marks I was getting from him would make up for the poor grades I was getting in math. I hoped Dad would look at it that way. I certainly did.

Gabriel was waiting for us when we got off the bus. It had stopped snowing. Bib had to practice piano this afternoon, so she strode ahead. I contemplated throwing a snowball at her, but resisted the temptation because if I missed I'd feel like a failure. Another *F*. It isn't just in school that you're graded, it's all through life.

"Did you have any luck with the snowflakes?" I asked Gabriel. "Any two the same?"

He said something that I deciphered as "They all melted."

"Well, next time put them in a shoe box filled with ice cubes," I told him. "That will keep the snowflakes cold, at least long enough for you to examine them and find the pair you are searching for."

I clumped into Quayles' house, hung my jacket up, and was immediately tempted to put it back on and go outside.

Hastings was screaming bloody murder in the kitchen while Mrs. Quayle made soothing noises. Bib was practicing scales on the piano in the living room. The houses up on Silvertree Hill Estates are all pretty small. It's not easy to escape a piano or a baby, or for that matter soothing noises. No wonder Gabriel had elected to play outside. Maybe I'd have to build an igloo to get away from the sound effects of our baby when Mom brought it home.

For a moment I considered going over to our house, but I might run into one of Dad's notes or even into Dad.

"I'm going to make some hot chocolate for all of you," said Mrs. Quayle. "And I baked a couple of batches of cookies this afternoon."

"Great," I said happily. After all, what's a little noise?

"And how nice that your father is joining us for dinner," she went on.

"You bet," I told her, less enthusiastically.

I walked into the living room and turned on the TV. I could get in some watching while Bib was playing the piano. She wasn't the only one who had something important to do, and there was so much noise already that no one could object to another decibel or two.

The only thing on was a dumb cartoon. (CARTOON, check.) I decided to work on the elephant riddle book while I was watching. I unrolled my sleeping bag and took out some paper and my pencils.

I wrote down another riddle:

> Why did the elephant wear a purple suit to school?
> *Because it matched his purple hat.*

I tried drawing different kinds of hats, and then I tried putting them on elephants.

In another minute, Mrs. Quayle was calling us to come out to the kitchen for hot chocolate and cookies. This was a pretty good way of life, I decided, now that things had quieted down. Mrs. Quayle spirited

Hastings off to his room, Bib went up to take another shower, and Gabriel and I kept eating cookies.

"Hot chocolate," I said to Gabriel as I sat at the counter. "Does that suggest anything to you?"

He looked at me.

"Our minds must keep searching for new ideas, new money-making schemes," I told him. "Sometimes the simplest ideas can lead to the greatest accomplishments. Hot chocolate is just one example, one possibility."

I ate a couple of cookies.

"As you have observed," I went on, "it is winter. The nights are very cold. How can you turn that to your advantage, you wonder. I will tell you."

Gabriel chewed steadily.

"You can put ice-cube trays out in the yard. The next time your mother makes hot chocolate, you can run outside and pour hot chocolate quickly into the empty trays. It would freeze so fast that you'd have ice cubes with hot chocolate inside. They'd sell like crazy. Something to warm you up while you waited for a bus, for instance. Cold on the outside, hot on the inside."

He kept looking at me, I kept talking. "As your business expanded, you could have a cart with a bell, drive all over town. Kids would come running out when

they'd hear you coming. Later, as you became even more successful, you could have a fleet of trucks. You'd be a millionaire. You'd never have to shake pennies out of a piggy bank again. You could hire someone to do that for you."

Gabriel and I polished off the cookies, and I thought I'd never be hungry again. That just goes to show: it takes a wise man to know his own stomach. By six o'clock I was starving.

Dad arrived at Quayles' all smiles and handshakes and out of breath, as if he'd just won the fifty-yard dash. He was happy about the baby, of course, and he was also excited about his plans for Weeble, Inc. He was going to put Weeble mattresses on the map. People who'd never heard of Weeble, Inc., maybe people who'd never heard of mattresses, were going to hear now.

As soon as anyone could get a word in edgewise, we all said how great it was about the baby and of course Dad acted as if he'd been solely responsible for its safe arrival. Mrs. Quayle murmured to Dad in a congratulatory sort of way as she took his coat, hung it up, and ushered him to a chair, promising him a glass of champagne to celebrate. I thought she was being the perfect hostess, but Bib whispered to me under her breath, "There she goes, acting deferential."

I didn't know what that meant, but whatever it was, it looked good to me, and I hoped I'd end up with someone who treated me like that instead of with someone like Bib who would probably turn out to be the ordering-around type, like "Hang up your own coat, stupid, and get me a glass of champagne, and incidentally, that's my chair you're occupying."

Seeing Dad relaxing in Mr. Quayle's chair was a cheerful novelty. Mrs. Quayle poured them each a glass of champagne which Hastings promptly knocked over. I could tell from Dad's expression that he disapproved of babies who acted like babies and that he thought the way Mrs. Quayle mopped up the champagne was inefficient. I knew he was going to offer some constructive criticism, and he would have and maybe he did, but Hastings started to cry and he drowned out anything Dad might have said or might be saying.

There was a flurry of activity, Hastings was put into his high chair and given more zwieback, and things finally settled down. Mrs. Quayle went back and forth to the dining room and the kitchen a couple of times, and I could see Dad counting her steps and working out a system for her that would save time. He reached into his jacket pocket, probably to take out his notebook, but he felt the cigars there and got sidetracked. "I'm passing these out to the men in the office," he said.

I glanced at Bib. "Just the men?" I asked, surprised. "We mustn't forget the women. After all, they are human beings, just like the rest of us, although we often forget that under the pressures of our workaday world."

Bib glared at me.

Dinner was ham and sweet potatoes, my favorite. I had three helpings of everything because I was storing up nourishment for the future. Besides, there wasn't anything else to do except listen to Dad. He was telling Mrs. Quayle everything she could possibly want to know about Weeble, Inc., and the Weeble mattresses and the big ad in the Sunday *New York Times* that Dad was working on so everyone would read about Weeble mattresses.

"A big full-page ad," murmured Mrs. Quayle. "Think of that. And in the Sunday *New York Times*. How exciting."

"It will make people aware of Weeble mattresses," said Dad. "Let me tell you about the ad. There will be a big photograph of Mr. Weeble himself. Under it the copy will read: *A Face You Can Trust.*" He paused, presumably waiting for applause. When none was forthcoming, he went on: *"A face you can trust,"* he repeated. *"A company you can rely on."*

"Oh, it's just lovely," said Mrs. Quayle, trying to get some sweet potatoes out of Hastings' hair.

"I've been running a contest," Dad went on. "A company contest. Everyone at Weeble has been trying to come up with a new slogan and a new logo. The best entries will each win one hundred dollars. It's an incentive to the whole company."

"What's a wogo?" whispered Gabriel, who was sitting next to me.

"Well, it's a sort of emblem," I whispered back. "A trademark. You know, like those stupid alligators that are on Bib's dumb T-shirts. It's a design. You're supposed to look at the logo and bang! You think of the product."

Of course I already knew about the contest. Every night after work Dad had been bringing home all of the logo and slogan suggestions, arranging them neatly on the kitchen counter, sorting them out, throwing away the ones he didn't want and saving the possible ones in a special envelope.

"And guess what happened this morning," he was saying.

"Oh, you had a new baby," said Mrs. Quayle, as Hastings dribbled disgustingly away. "That's very exciting, isn't it, children?"

Dad cleared his throat. "Well, of course, the baby. But something else. This morning when I left the hospital I came home and I went over all the latest drawings that had been submitted for a new logo." He paused importantly. "And among those drawings, I found it. The right logo." He smiled expansively. "I knew someone in the company would come up with one. The company that works together, works." Another of his sayings. Maybe he could put them all in a book, get famous.

He smiled around the table. "The winning logo represents the sleeping public. You see it, and bingo, you think about mattresses, Weeble mattresses. It's perfect. Now all we need is the right slogan."

He kept talking and Mrs. Quayle kept making soothing noises, whether to quiet Hastings or Dad, I wasn't sure.

Weeble, Inc.'s present slogan was *We stand behind each mattress,* and their logo was a big red *W* with little wings on the top of the *W*. At least it was supposed to be wings. Actually, it looked like little sprouts of hair.

Mrs. Quayle murmured pleasantly as she wiped up the milk that Hastings had spilled. "I just love contests," she said.

"Of course, it's only open to Weeble personnel and their families," said Dad. "Otherwise, I'd be happy to welcome any suggestions of yours."

"Oh, I haven't any suggestions," said Mrs. Quayle.

"I was just thinking that your idea of a contest was a very good one."

Bib whispered in my ear, "See?"

I guess she was back on that deferential bit again.

"I didn't bake a cake or a pie today," Mrs. Quayle said apologetically, as Bib rolled her eyes. "We'll just have to take potluck. Whatever is in the freezer will have to do, I'm afraid. Roberta, dear, will you please bring us some ice cream and chocolate sauce, there's a dear." It always seemed funny to me to hear her called Roberta.

Bib sent me a meaningful glance, which might mean anything. Maybe it meant, come and help me. Maybe it meant, I'll never spend *my* life being a housewife. Maybe it meant, you have sweet potatoes on your chin. You never knew, with Bib's meaningful glances.

Dad kept talking about Weeble, Inc., and how many mattresses they'd sell after people saw the full-page ad, while Gabriel tilted dangerously on his chair. Hastings was trying to swallow his hand. Maybe he was going to eat himself up. That would be all right with me.

In a few minutes Bib served the dessert. The ice-cream ball on my plate looked suspiciously like a snowball. I bit into it. It was. Gabriel must have taken my advice and stored his snowballs in the freezer for future reference.

I glanced around the table. No one else seemed to notice. Actually, it wasn't bad. I guess anything tastes all right if it's covered with chocolate sauce.

(9)

If You've Seen One Baby, You've Seen Them All

After dinner, Dad drove me over to the hospital so we could see Mom and the new baby. Babies behind glass: the best kind. The ones that weren't sleeping were crying, and nurses were going around doing mysterious, useful things for them.

All the babies were in little plastic see-through bassinets, and Dad pointed out one of the crying babies and said, "There she is." I couldn't see much of her besides her open mouth. I hoped it would be closed by the time she got home.

Fastened to the bassinets were name cards, blue for boys, pink for girls, just as there were blankets in the appropriate colors. I wondered what Bib would think of that. She'd probably make a scene, insist that they all be the same color.

Dad was still standing there, maybe trying to figure out how many days it would be before the baby would be old enough to help shovel the snow or mow the grass. There was nothing to do, so I started to read the little cards on the bassinets. I noticed that our baby's card read *Janet Clegg,* so I knew we'd been admiring the wrong baby. I looked around and finally spotted the card that read *Leslie Laura Langren,* and since the open mouth in that bassinet looked just like the one Dad had pointed out, I didn't say anything. If you've seen one baby, you've seen them all.

I thought Dad was just admiring the (wrong) baby all that time, but when I looked over at him I saw that he had taken out his little pocket notebook and his stopwatch. So he was timing something. Timing what, I wondered. Maybe the intervals between crying spells, although so far there hadn't been any. He was marking things down, making diagrams, nodding his head energetically.

Finally he nodded with satisfaction, returned the notebook to his pocket, and we proceeded down the hall to Mom's room. Dad said he had to go downstairs for a minute to pick up some things for Mom at the hospital gift shop. "She brought the wrong bag," he explained, and Mom winked at me. He doesn't like to take the blame for anything.

I looked around and saw my bag of comic books on the floor. Good. I'd have something to read.

Mom looked just the same except that her hair was frizzier and her stomach was flatter. "What do you think of the baby?" she asked.

"Beautiful," I lied. "A real prize."

We talked for a couple of minutes about the baby. There's just so much conversation you can have about a baby that's just been born: general appearance, gender, weight, length, color (or existence) of hair. We were just getting to the hair when a nurse came in and said I'd have to wait in the waiting room down the hall because they were going to be bringing the baby in to Mom.

I told Mom I'd see her in a couple of days, and I headed out of the room, picking up my bag of comic books on the way. I'd already read every one of them several times, of course, but it was like seeing something on rerun: familiar.

I was in the waiting room reading my third comic when someone wearing a pale blue surgical gown and mask and cap walked into the waiting room. When he saw me, he said, "We meet again. We never know

what chance encounters fate may have in store for us."

He took off the mask and cap, and I saw that it was Bruce Dooster. Maybe he delivered babies on the side: I wouldn't have been surprised, because he certainly did everything else. I found out last summer, when he'd been painting our house, that he did a lot of other things, too. I noticed that there was a strap around his neck and at the end of the strap a big camera. I remembered now that he'd told me once that in addition to his other interests and professions, he was a photographer.

He patted his camera. "New beginnings," he said. "A photograph of a baby: a record of the very beginning of a life that has not been lived before and will not be lived again."

Well, if he'd taken a picture of our new baby, I hoped the tonsils were in focus.

He glanced at the bag of comic books on the floor.

"It's gratifying to see that you carry with you something to read, rather than depending on the material provided in the hospital waiting room, always a gamble. I am further pleased to note that your selection of literature is just what we have been studying in class. My words, then, on the role of comic books in American Literature were not for naught."

He put the mask and the cap back on. "New faces

to photograph, new worlds to conquer, new seas to sail. That's the principal thing about babies: there's always another one coming along."

At that moment Dad arrived on the scene, out of breath, as usual.

Dad had met Bruce Dooster before, but I was sure he wouldn't recognize him with the surgical mask. He didn't.

"Doctor," said Dad, "I've worked out a far more efficient schedule for the nurses to care for the newborns. If the nurses move counterclockwise, and proceed down the third aisle to—"

Bruce Dooster didn't say anything, maybe because it was hard to talk through the mask—maybe because it was hard to talk through one of Dad's conversations.

"I haven't time to work out all the little details," Dad went on, "but here's the general idea." He ripped a page out of his notebook and handed it to Bruce Dooster. "You may want to bring this up at the next staff meeting."

"Counterclockwise," said Bruce Dooster. "Brilliant."

"It's usually impossible to see the problem closest to you," said Dad modestly. "It takes an expert from the outside to get to the bottom of things. Let me give you my card." He presented one with a flourish. I'd seen the card before:

WALTER J. LANGREN

WEEBLE, INC.

WE STAND BEHIND EACH MATTRESS

"We stand behind each mattress," read Bruce Dooster aloud. "What an alarming thought." He pursed his lips. "Walter J. Langren? No relation to Noah Langren of Mulberry School, by chance?"

Dad stared at him for a moment, then he turned to me. "I knew something funny was going on over at school." To Bruce Dooster, he said, "Tell me, Doctor, it's always best to hear the truth, however painful the truth might be."

"Your son, eh?" asked Bruce Dooster in mock surprise. He'd met Dad before, last summer, and for some relationships once is enough.

"I can readily see that Noah here is a chip off the old block. No slouch, you know, when it comes to figuring out shortcuts. Yes, you have every reason to be proud. Look at him, carrying his work with him even on a hospital visit, just as you carry your work along wherever you go. It's easy to see that he has assimilated your own concept of never wasting time." He reached in his pocket. "Congratulations. Have a cigar."

Dad blinked and took it. Bruce Dooster saluted and strode out of the waiting room.

(10)

Sort of Like Your Friendly Neighborhood Undertaker

Dad didn't say much on the way home, which was far from his usual habit. Maybe he was just sorting through all of the things that were on his mind: the baby, the big advertisement for Weeble, Inc. in *The New York Times*, my (imagined) problems at school, and this most recent revelation, which was that I was a chip off the old block. That must have come as a total surprise because it was probably the first time in my life that he'd heard anything good about me. Not that he'd ever heard anything bad, really: it's just that I was very rarely the subject of any conversation at all.

Dad stopped to drop me off at Quayles'. He was

going home to work on the ad. "Working after the working day is the way to get ahead," he said. As I've said, Dad has lots of sayings like that, good advice in little capsules, like medicine.

"I've got a lot of homework to do, too," I told him, thinking of the television evening ahead.

"That's very important," he said. "And so is a good night's rest, of course. Go to bed early, Noah. A good night's sleep means a good day's work."

"That would be a good slogan for Weeble, Inc.," I said, getting out of the car. *"A good night means a good day."*

"That's it," said Dad excitedly. *"A good night means a good day. Sleep on a Weeble mattress tonight.* It's just what I was looking for." He paused awkwardly. "Thank you, Noah."

"Well, it was your saying," I said modestly.

"I've got the logo, now I've got the slogan, and Mr. Weeble's photograph will be ready in a few days. Then we're ready to roll."

I was ready to roll myself. I said good night again and made my way across the snow to Quayles' back-door.

My stomach and I were getting pretty used to living here, and I knew it would be a shock to my system when it came time to move back home.

It was.

Mom came home on Sunday with the baby: instant chaos. I couldn't figure out how one small baby could take up so much space. Or make so much noise.

And Mom, never very wide awake in the morning, was even less so now because she wasn't getting much sleep at night. "I'm afraid I'll be so sleepy one of these days that I'll just throw the baby out with the bathwater," she said.

Since she wasn't working and Dad was, he'd borrowed the earplugs she used to wear when she was studying for her degree so he could sleep through all the racket.

"You can sleep during the day," he told her.

"Tell the baby," said Mom.

Dad's latest time-saving idea was that we should have TV dinners every night until we got squared away. At the rate we were going, that would be about ten years.

Now that I was back in the house again, Dad was reminded of some of the jobs he'd had in mind for me to do.

"Noah," he said, that second night, "I left a note that I wanted you to sweep the garage."

"Oh, that," I said. "Well, I saw the note, but I couldn't read your writing."

"Couldn't read my writing?" asked Dad, his eyebrows shooting up. "The note was typed, Noah."

"So it was," I said, thinking quickly. "What I meant was that I couldn't read it because I couldn't find my glasses. And I couldn't see them without them and so I—"

"Well, see that it's taken care of," interrupted Dad.

I'd already thought of my next excuse: The cars were in the garage, so I couldn't really do a good job on the floor.

I walked into the house on Tuesday after school, all set to start watching TV. The set had been fixed. Dad had been to market, so at least there would be stacks of TV dinners and some stuff to make sandwiches with. It wasn't gourmet, but it would probably keep me from starving to death.

Mom was walking up and down with the baby, who had surprisingly and mercifully fallen asleep.

"Look," said Mom, "sleeping like a baby."

"I thought so," I said. "I could hear all this quiet a block away."

"Well, I just fed her. Again. Food works miracles, they say. Not always, but sometimes. Not often, but seldom. Here, you hold her while I run through a load of laundry."

Me hold her!

"I don't know how," I told her.

"There's nothing to it. All you need is a lap. Sit down. See, now you've got one." She plunked the baby into my arms and went down to the basement.

I was afraid to breathe. I'd had no idea she'd feel so small. I sat there until my arm went to sleep, and then I had to change position. I tried breathing a little, too. She opened her eyes.

I'd read somewhere that babies don't really see when they're so young, but I'd swear she was looking at me, sizing me up, wondering what I'd be like.

"Hey," I said, "it's okay. I'm okay. Honest. Don't cry, for pete's sake."

I was so busy holding her that I forgot I was starving to death, but I remembered the minute Mom came back in and took her to the nursery. I fixed myself a bologna sandwich with mayonnaise, poured myself a glass of milk, and walked into the living room to turn on the set.

"Good heavens," said Mom when she came in. "Daytime television. What will they think of next?"

"It's homework," I explained. "My assignment in American Literature is to watch all the television I can so that I can understand everything about it because it has such an important influence on our lives."

"I didn't know there was anything good on in the afternoon," she said.

"There isn't," I told her, "but it doesn't matter. I have to familiarize myself with the medium."

"What's the world coming to?" asked Mom.

The one channel we could get had an excruciatingly long boring interview with someone who was an expert in crop rotation in Afghanistan or Timbuktu or somewhere.

"A program like this could put you to sleep faster than a Weeble mattress," said Mom in a few minutes. She yawned and stretched. "I'm going to take a bubble bath while I can," she said. "Listen for the baby, will you? And pick her up if she cries."

"No problem," I said proudly. It wouldn't be long before Leslie Laura would be counting on me, looking forward to seeing me. I'd be popular. I'd be important. I'd be needed.

When Dad arrived a couple of programs later, it was in a flurry of importance. He had picked up from the photographer the "definitive" photograph of Mr. Weeble, and it was going to be delivered to *The New York Times* advertising department immediately. In fact, a messenger from Weeble was coming tonight to pick it up and take it to the newspaper. The rest of the ad had been ready and there for a couple of days.

"It's done and I've done it," said Dad proudly. "This ad will change the fortunes of Weeble, Inc., and I'll have been totally responsible. Mr. Weeble has left everything in my hands. He'll be in for a very pleasant surprise when he sees the ad, you can be sure."

Dad took the photograph of Mr. Weeble out of the envelope. A round sincere face with glasses to match. Even his hair, which was parted in the middle, looked sincere, sort of like your friendly neighborhood undertaker. Someone you'd vote for if he were running for something.

"A face you can rely on," said Dad reverently. "A company you can trust."

He put the picture back into the envelope, and I pictured Mr. Weeble still glowing sincerely inside.

Then Leslie Laura started to cry. She had a very loud voice for a very small baby, and it was all we could do to get our TV dinners organized, in the oven, and down our throats in all the confusion.

"It's her bedtime," announced Dad firmly. "You simply have to get her on a schedule. A routine. It's as easy as that. She'll learn quickly when it's time to sleep and time to eat and time to be awake and which is which."

"You tell her," suggested Mom.

"You're too soft," Dad told her. "Picking her up

every time she cries. Feeding her every few minutes. She'll never learn that way. She has to stay on schedule. She has to know what's what. Here, give her to me. I'll get her settled. Babies prefer routine. They *like* it. It's the only way they can figure things out."

Dad marched off to the nursery with Leslie Laura just as the doorbell rang.

"That will be the messenger," called Dad over his shoulder. "Give him the photograph of Mr. Weeble. It's there on the kitchen counter."

As was just about everything else: TV dinner trays, napkins, forks, empty glasses, pencils, bottles, and the evening paper.

There. I found the envelope. I grabbed it, ran to the door, and handed it to the messenger.

Dad didn't seem to be having much luck with the baby's new routine, at least the noise level was extremely high.

"I think she's hungry," said Dad finally, coming back to the kitchen.

"She usually is," said Mom.

Well, then, Leslie Laura and I had a lot in common.

I decided to fix myself a sandwich. In a year or so, I'd be fixing one for her, too.

(11)

Anything Is Possible

There are good days and bad days. The thing is you can't tell which is going to be which ahead of time.

"I've invited the Quayles over tonight after supper," said Mom over our TV dinners that Saturday. "They haven't seen the baby yet. And besides, it's Bib's birthday, remember?"

How could I forget? She talked about it all the time. About how old she was getting, and about how much she wanted the skateboard she *wasn't* getting, and how time was flying by and life was practically *over*.

I didn't have a present for her. I really wanted to give her something so she'd give me something for my birthday. I'd finished the riddle book *(What Are These Elephants Doing in This Book?)* and had stapled it neatly together. I could always give her that. A first edition. It might be worth thousands of dollars in time to come.

"We'll have cookies and punch," Mom went on. "They're going to be having her cake at home."

"Fine, fine," said Dad, who was feeling very expansive lately, now that the ad was finished. He'd be happy to have a new audience to brag to. Maybe he'd hand out cigars.

When the Quayles arrived, there seemed to be more of them, or else they took up more room or something. For one thing, Mr. Quayle had just come back from his business trip and for another, Bib had grown at least three inches since yesterday. Maybe she *was* a year older, suddenly. Maybe she was going through a growing spurt or maybe she just looked so much taller because she'd piled her hair on top of her head where it balanced precariously.

Their big excitement was that Hastings had learned to say Mommy and Daddy. Actually, he called *everybody* either Mamma or Dadda, depending on their gender. I wondered if Bib thought that having different names for parents was discriminating. Maybe there should be one name for both, like Bunna.

They all peered at Leslie Laura and said kind things, and I felt pretty proud, as if she was my doing.

"How's it going?" whispered Bib.

"Okay," I said. "She cries a lot."

"The baby?"

"No, Mom."

"Well," she said consolingly, "things will get better as time goes by."

"They'd better get better," I said. "Dad can't understand why the baby can't get on a schedule. I've never heard so much yelling."

"Your dad?"

"No, the baby. By the way, Happy Birthday. Did you get anything you wanted?"

"All I really got was older," said Bib with a sigh. "Gabriel gave me an empty secondhand rusty bird cage. For the canaries he's going to be giving me, he said."

Well, I could give her the riddle book. But I hadn't wrapped it. And besides, the more I thought about it, the more it didn't seem like the sort of present anyone would want. After all, it was just a bunch of stupid riddles with dumb drawings. I never did get the hippopotamus in the bathtub right.

"This is such a darling stage," cooed Mrs. Quayle, holding Leslie Laura. "It's too bad it's over so quickly."

Mom nodded. "Yes, she's changed a lot even since

she was born. Luckily, we have a beautiful picture of her, taken that very first day. There was such a nice photographer at the hospital. Noah, it's right there in an envelope on the kitchen counter. I'm sure everyone would like to see it. It's so sweet, I've ordered more."

I found a big flat envelope out in the kitchen and carried it in. "Do show the Quayles, dear," said Mom. "I'll get the cookies and punch ready."

"I'll help," said Bib. Show-off. Gabriel followed them out to the kitchen, presumably to get a head start on the cookies.

I took the picture out of the envelope, turned it over, and found myself looking at Mr. Weeble, who was in turn looking sincerely at me. It took me a couple of minutes to react. If Mr. Weeble's picture was here, then what had gone off with the messenger the other day?

There was only one possibility: I had given that messenger the picture of Leslie Laura by mistake. I sat down, hard. Since all the chairs were occupied, that meant that I sat on the floor. I would have liked to have cut a hole in it and crawled in.

Dad was explaining to Mr. Quayle all about the ad that was to appear in tomorrow's *New York Times*. "I'll drive into town first thing in the morning, get a copy," he said. "In this town you can never get it a day ahead, the way you can in the city."

"It so happens that I've just come back from New York," said Mr. Quayle. "I brought the early edition of the Sunday *Times* back with me on the plane. Why don't I just run over and get it now?"

Now? O, wow. This must be what death row was like.

"Wonderful," said Dad. "That way I can see the ad tonight instead of having to wait until tomorrow."

Dad was electrified with excitement, whereas I felt that I had already been electrocuted.

"Oh, this will make it a triple celebration," said Mrs. Quayle, patting Leslie Laura gently. "We're all together for Roberta's birthday, for the new baby, and for the ad, too. Three things to celebrate."

Mr. Quayle stood up cheerfully. He was probably glad to have an excuse to get away from Dad for a minute. Since his coat was hanging in the front hall, he left by the front door. I'd have to figure out a way to keep him from getting back in.

"Dadda," said Hastings, crawling over to Dad.

I was hoping that Mr. Quayle would become snowbound or get hopelessly lost between our house and theirs, when the doorbell rang.

"It must be Mr. Quayle, back again," I said quickly. "I'll get it."

Maybe I could grab the paper from him and hide it. Maybe I could send him away under some clever pretext.

I threw the door open, prepared to tell Mr. Quayle that we had a fire in the kitchen and we all had to evacuate the premises.

It was Bruce Dooster. "Aha," he said. "Another fateful encounter." He handed me an envelope. "The extra prints your mother ordered of the baby." I took the envelope.

Mom came to the door, Bib behind her, carrying Hastings.

"Who is it?" called Dad.

We all spoke at once.

"It's our American Literature teacher," said Bib.

"It's that nice photographer," said Mom.

"It's the doctor who gave you the cigar," I said.

"Dadda," said Hastings.

"Do come in," said Mom to Bruce Dooster. "I want to give you a check for these pictures."

Bruce Dooster walked into the living room and looked around. "Well, well, a population explosion," he said.

Maybe his presence would get Dad's mind off getting that copy of *The New York Times*. No such luck.

"Where's Quayle?" Dad asked. "And who are all these people coming to the door?" He looked accusingly at Bruce Dooster. "I thought you were going to be someone else," he said.

"I myself often hope that will prove to be the case," said Bruce Dooster.

The doorbell. This time it had to be Mr. Quayle. I'd use the fire-in-the-kitchen ruse to get him away.

I couldn't believe it, but it was Grace, the bus driver. My whole life must be flashing before my eyes as I went down for the last time.

"Come in, Quayle," shouted Dad.

"It must be the newsboy collecting," Mom suggested, as she came in from the kitchen.

"Newsperson," said Bib.

Grace spoke up. "I'm your Avon representative. May I come in?"

"Is that Quayle?" called Dad impatiently.

"It's the newsperson," said Bib over her shoulder to Dad.

She hadn't seen Grace yet.

"It's the Avon lady," said Mom.

"It's the bus driveress," I said.

"Mamma," said Hastings.

"Why are all these women coming to the door at this hour? Where's Quayle? I want that paper," said Dad.

The next doorbell had to be Mr. Quayle. It was. I

was just taking a breath to tell him about the problem in the kitchen when Dad raced to the door and took the paper out of his hands. He set it on the coffee table in the living room and started to leaf through it, looking for the Weeble ad. I knew the paper had a travel section, and I was wondering whether they had a special price on a one-way trip to Siberia.

Mom invited Grace and Bruce Dooster to stay for cookies, our baby started to cry, Hastings pulled a lamp over, and everyone was crowded together in the living room with some spillover into the kitchen, all talking at once.

Leafing through the pages of *The New York Times,* Dad finally came to the Weeble ad. It was a huge, life-sized picture of Leslie Laura, yawning. *A Face You Can Trust.*

I shut my eyes. I had seen enough. And I had probably seen enough of my life, too, I decided.

In spite of the volume of noise, it was easy for me to hear Dad. It was a combination of vowels and consonants I had never heard before.

Help! I'd really be in trouble now.

Over all the other sounds was another: the telephone. Mom, fussing around in the kitchen, had no way of knowing about the wrong picture being in the ad, so she was oblivious to disaster.

She called Dad. "Darling, it's Mr. Weeble on the phone."

Dad blanched.

I wondered whether the Quayles would be willing to adopt me. The bustle and confusion around me sounded like a funeral dirge. My own personal funeral.

I couldn't hear Dad on the telephone with all the other confusion. He'd probably been struck speechless. I wondered whether I could sneak up to my room, pack a couple of pillowcases with my earthly possessions, and flee.

For a moment the noise level subsided: everyone was eating cookies and drinking punch. I was paralyzed with indecision. Run outside, then pack? Pack first?

Dad came back into the living room. "I don't believe it," he said. "That was Mr. Weeble. He's seen the ad. He loves it. Says it's original, eye-catching. Thinks I'm a genius."

Dad shook his head unbelievingly.

"Oh, that's nice, dear," said Mom, holding Leslie Laura and patting her on the back.

"Hey, what's this?"

It was Bib, leafing through my elephant riddle book.

"These are terrific drawings. Funny! Great!"

Hey, she liked it!

I cleared my throat. "Oh, it's just something I

whipped up for your birthday," I told her. "I haven't had a chance to wrap it."

She continued to look at it, turning the pages and smiling. "Noah, it's marvelous."

I felt as if I'd just got an *A* for the semester.

Dad was still shaking his head. "Mr. Weeble likes it!" he said. "Likes it!" He picked up the ad to look at it again. Then he turned to me. "Noah, I've been thinking. The slogan: *A good night means a good day*. It's really yours, you know. So by rights the prize money is yours, too."

A hundred dollars! I was rich! Richer than I'd ever been or probably than I ever would be.

I felt like a hero. I *was* a hero.

As soon as I could get near it, I picked up the ad and examined it. Leslie Laura's yawn was contagious: I yawned, too, but not from sleepiness. From excitement.

At the bottom of the page was the new Weeble trademark, the new logo that Dad had said represented the sleeping public. At first I thought it was my drawing of the hippopotamus in the bathtub. I looked closer. It was. Dad must have seen it on the kitchen counter and thought it was one of the suggestions from the suggestion box.

Bib and Gabriel came up behind me to look at the ad.

"That's my logo. I drew it," I said proudly. "I just won another hundred dollars."

Bib opened her mouth to say something, but I beat her to it. "It's just the way I've always said," I went on. "Anything is possible. All it takes is a little confidence."

Bib was wide-eyed.

"That skateboard you wanted?" I said casually to her. "It's yours. We'll go down and pick it out tomorrow, okay?" I hesitated. "In fact, we'll both get one. I'll learn how, too. After all, you can't learn anything without trying."

She just stared at me. This time with respect.

Suddenly I felt taller. Maybe I was, and maybe it was only because Bib's hair had come down.

"Gowwy gee wiwwikers," said Gabriel.

Leslie Laura started to cry.

"I'll take care of her," I said grandly.

It was true, what I'd said. Anything is possible. All it takes is a little confidence.

ABOUT THE AUTHOR

FLORENCE PARRY HEIDE, a resident of Kenosha, Wisconsin, is the author of many humorous children's books, including *The Shrinking of Treehorn*, *Treehorn's Treasure*, *Treehorn's Wish*, *Banana Twist*, and *Banana Blitz*.

ABOUT THE ILLUSTRATOR

MARYLIN HAFNER, a talented artist who lives in Cambridge, Massachusetts, also provided the illustrations for *Time's Up!*, an A.L.A. Notable Book.